Disney's **Doug**™

Created by Jim Jinkins

CHRONICLES

A Day with Dirtbike

Lisa Goldman and Linda K. Garvey

Illustrated by
Matthew C. Peters, Jeffrey Nodelman, Vinh Truong, Brian
Donnelly, and Sophie Kittredge

A Day with Dirtbike is hand-illustrated by
the same Grade A Quality Jumbo artists
who bring you *Disney's Doug*, the television series.

New York

Original characters for "The Funnies" developed by Jim Jinkins and
Joé Aaron.

Printed in the United States of America.

1 3 5 7 9 10 8 6 4 2

The artwork for this book is prepared using watercolor.

The text for this book is set in 18-point Century Schoolbook.

Library of Congress Catalog Card Number: 97-80217

ISBN:0-7868-4233-4

Created by
Jim Jinkins

A Day
with Dirtbike

CHAPTER ONE

Doug Funnie let out a huge
sneeze as he and Porkchop sat
down in front of the television,
holding drinks and a huge bowl of
buttered popcorn.

"Bless you, dear," said Theda,
writing at her desk.

"Thanks, Mom," Doug said. At
his feet, seven-month-old

Cleopatra Dirtbike gurgled something that sounded like, "Eh, Duh!" Was she trying to say "Hey, Doug!" he wondered? Probably not. She was wrestling with her stuffed moose.

Doug was watching his favorite show—*Dr. Cop!* He was the coolest!

The telephone rang beside Doug. "Douglas, would you get that, please?" his mother asked. Doug didn't move. Dr. Cop had cornered a hardened criminal in a pet shop, and the guy had a severe allergic reaction. Now Dr. Cop was giving him CPR while handcuffing him. With a sigh,

Theda got up to answer the phone.

"Hello? Oh, hi, Mom!" Theda said. "What, dear? I can't hear you. Hold on. I'll go to a quieter phone," she shouted to Doug's Grandma Opal.

"Douglas," she said, shaking his shoulder. "Please hang up when I tell you to. And watch Dirtbike." She shook his shoulder again. "Douglas, are you listening?"

"Sure, Mom. Uh, hang up the phone. Okay, sure . . ."

Doug said without taking his eyes off the screen. He took the receiver and hooked it over his leg. He and Porkchop both reached for the popcorn at the same time.

A minute later, Cleopatra Dirtbike took the receiver off Doug's knee. She held it up and began to speak into the earpiece. "A-Day!" she said to Grandma

Opal and Theda. Then she dropped the receiver on the floor.

"Douglas! Douglas?" Theda's voice sounded small through the phone line.

Turning to the popcorn, Dirtbike put one kernel in her mouth, and another, and another. Soon her mouth was full.

"Doug! What are you doing? Hang up the—HAVE YOU LOST YOUR MIND??!!!" Doug's older sister, Judy, shouted.

She quickly grabbed the baby with one hand and said, "No!" firmly. Then she scooped the popcorn from Dirtbike's mouth with her other hand.

Dirtbike opened her mouth and began to wail at the top of her lungs.

That got Doug's attention. He was positive he had done nothing wrong. And now he was missing the best part of the show! "What'd I do? Me and Porkchop were just sitting here watching—"

Judy cut him off. "You were just about to let our precious baby sister choke to death on that popcorn, that's what you were doing! Doug, how could you do that to Cleopatra?" she said.

"Her name's Dirtbike, Judy. That's what *I* named her."

"Well, *I* named her Cleopatra, and that's beside the point!"

By that time, Dirtbike's howls and Judy's yelling had brought Dad into the room. "Doug! Judy! What's going on in here?"

For a moment, chaos ruled and Porkchop covered his ears with his paws.

Then Phil took over. "Quiet! Everybody, be quiet!"

At that moment, Theda joined

them. "Is everything all right?" she asked.

"Yes, dear," Phil answered. "I'm about to get to the bottom of this." He turned to Judy and Doug. "All right, what's this all about?"

Doug and Judy started talking at the same time.

"Well, she came in the room yelling while I was—"

"He was about to let—"

"Hold it! One at a time! And no yelling, please! Now," Phil said, "what happened? Judy, you go first."

"But, Dad!" Doug protested. "She always—"

"Doug, Judy will go first." Dad was out of patience.

Judy made a face at Doug and began. "Well, Mom asked me to hang up the phone," she said, pointing to the receiver at Doug's feet.

He sheepishly hung it in its place.

Judy continued, "Doug was *supposed* to do it, but you know how he is when he watches that tasteless barbaric action-adventure drivel he loves!"

Doug cut Judy a mean look as she continued. "Mom was talking to Grandma Opal and she couldn't even hear her above the *Dr. Cop* noise coming through the phone! I came in here and what did I find!?" she went on. "*This* irresponsible, uncaring, TV-watching—"

"Judy, that's enough drama. Just tell us what happened," Dad cut her off.

Whew! Doug thought. It's a good thing Dad understands how

she is when she gets worked up!

Judy continued in horrified tones, "So, as I walked in, Cleopatra was cramming a fistful of POPCORN into her mouth!"

Phil looked at Theda. "Oh, my!" she said. "Douglas, you must never give popcorn to babies. It can choke them."

"But I didn't know! Besides, I didn't *give* it to her," Doug said. "She just took it."

"Doug," Dad said. "She's a baby. You are responsible for her when she's left in your care."

"But—," Doug started.

"And, Douglas," Mom chimed in. "I *did* ask you to watch her while

I was on the phone with
Grandma Opal."

A thought hit her suddenly.
"Oh! Grandma Opal! I almost
forgot!"

CHAPTER TWO

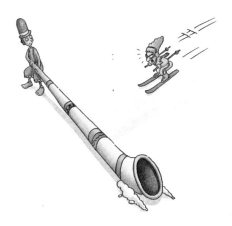

Theda became serious. "We have a little problem. You know your Grandma Opal went skiing in Yakestonia."

Everyone nodded. Grandma Opal's motto was "*You gotta live, LIVE, **LIVE!***" She was good at it, too.

"Well," Mom continued, "she was

coming to the bottom of a slope when one of those traditional Yak horn-blowers came out dragging his horn. Mom couldn't stop herself in time, and she fell over it, spraining her ankle. I'm going to bring her here to recuperate. Her flight arrives tomorrow in Bloatsburg, so I need someone to baby-sit Dirtbike while I go pick her up at the airport."

"Well, I can't do it," said Judy. "I have tickets to see Derek Derekson in 'Shakespeare on Ice' tomorrow! I've had these tickets for months!"

Everyone looked at Doug.

"M-m-m-me?" he asked.

"What do you think, Phil?" Theda asked.

"I'd do it myself, but you know Saturday *is* my biggest day at the Busy Beaver. No," Phil said with finality. "Judy will have to take care of Dirtbike this time."

"But, Dad," Judy whined. "Can't Doug do it alone? He's big now! He's responsible! He baby-sits Skeeter's little brother, Dale. I ALWAYS have to baby-sit! I even had to baby-sit for Doug! It's not fair!"

"How can you even suggest that, after what just happened, Judy?" her dad asked. "Doug didn't even know about the popcorn. Besides, Dale's a lot older than Dirtbike. No, we need someone with your experience."

Doug just sat there, amazed. It looked as if he would get off scot-free. He had big plans for tomorrow, too. He and Skeeter had some important goofing off to do at the mall.

Dad continued, "But I do think Doug should stay here to help you out. It will help him practice being responsible for when he does baby-sit solo."

"But, Daaaad," Doug whined.

"Sorry, Doug, but your mother and I need you to cooperate with Judy tomorrow so we can take

care of Grandma. It's a family
emergency."

"I'll be baby-sitting for the rest
of my life," Judy grumbled as she
left the den.

CHAPTER THREE

A few minutes later, Doug opened the door to his room. Suddenly, Judy leaped into the doorway, blocking Doug and Porkchop.

"Judy, what are you doing?" Doug asked.

"I'm getting your attention in a dramatic way, little brother," she replied.

"Well, why do you always have to be so weird?" Doug asked, annoyed.

"Is twenty dollars weird?" she asked.

"Welllll . . . it depends on what I have to do for it," Doug answered.

"Baby-sit for me tomorrow," she said.

"No way, Judy. You heard Dad. *You* have to." Doug was not falling for any of Judy's tricks.

"But Dougie," she pleaded. "I've waited months for this day! Derek Derekson in 'Shakespeare on Ice'! Besides, Cleopatra is a breeze to take care of."

"We'll be in BIG trouble if Mom

and Dad find out! I could use the money, but it's not worth it, just so you can make goo-goo eyes at some goofy guy in tights."

"How about thirty dollars? Would it be worth that?" Judy wasn't giving up.

"Wow! You *are* desperate!" Doug said.

"Thirty-five?" Judy replied. "And that's my final offer. Going . . . going . . ."

That was too much to resist. "Okay," Doug told her, "as long as you come back as *soon* as it's over!"

"Well, of course, silly. I don't want to get caught either." Then

Judy quickly took charge
again.

"Besides, you've got to take
responsibility! Promise me you
won't mess this up, or . . . I get to
read your journal."

"Wait a minute! I don't want to
do this at all! The deal's off!"
Doug was no dummy.

"Okay, okay! But you better make sure you don't mess this up for me, or . . . else!" Judy finished lamely.

As a parting shot she said, "You know, Dougie, it's your turn to watch Cleopatra, anyway. I baby-sat you."

"It's not *my* fault you were born first!" Doug replied.

Judy continued, "And I was good to you. I could have made your life miserable, but—"

"You *did*!" Doug cried. "Remember the time you tried to fly me like a kite during a thunderstorm? *And* the time you were Captain Ahab and I had to be

Moby Dick? You tried to harpoon me with a toilet plunger!"

"Oh, pish-posh! Merely the enthusiasm of youth! Who could have guided your faltering steps toward manhood—well, boy-hood—better than I?" With a theatrical flourish, she turned and was gone.

Doug and Porkchop looked at each other in disbelief. "Roger! Stinky! This chair!" Doug yelled after her. "*Anybody* would have been better!"

CHAPTER FOUR

Saturday morning, Judy was
holding Dirtbike while Doug
waved good-bye to Mom and Dad.
When they were out of sight,
Judy turned to Doug and said,
"Okay, time for a crash course in
baby-sitting."

"What? I can do this! All I have

to do is keep her from getting hurt!" he replied.

"Well, you're a whiz at that!" she taunted him. "Remember the popcorn?"

"I didn't know about that! Now, I do!" he came back. "I can do this," he said.

"Dougie, Cleopatra's a handful," Judy cautioned.

"I thought you said she's a breeze," Doug countered.

"Okay, okay. Let me just give you one piece of advice. One: never take Cleopatra where you cannot have complete control. So don't leave the house. Are you listening, Doug?" she asked him.

"Don't leave home," Doug repeated.

"Now let me see you change that diaper," Judy added.

"No way!" protested Doug. "She doesn't need one now."

"But you've never done it before," Judy said.

Porkchop paraded by them in a towel tied like a diaper.

"And I'm NOT doing it one more time than I have to!" Doug exclaimed.

"Okay, Mr. Expert Baby-sitter." Judy shrugged and handed Doug a long piece of paper. "These are emergency phone numbers. And this," she said, pulling a twenty dollar bill from her pocket, "is emergency money Mom gave me just in case.

"Now, I'm off to the show," she said. "Good luck!"

"Don't worry. I've got it all under control," Doug told her. He waved good-bye. The moment she was gone, Dirtbike began to cry.

CHAPTER FIVE

Doug and Porkchop took Dirtbike into the house. Soon, she was happily playing and Doug said, "Well, what do ya know, Porkchop? I *am* good at this!"

They played Wrestle the Moose, Peek-a-Boo, Pop Goes the Weasel, and Where's Dirtbike's Nose? Doug even did a little dance with his baby sister and Porkchop. But fifteen minutes after Judy had left, Dirtbike was tired of all of those games, and Doug was out of ideas.

She whimpered. Doug made faces and funny noises. That worked for about thirty seconds. Then she started to cry for real.

A bottle! Why didn't I think of that sooner? Doug thought.

The bottle worked. Dirtbike cuddled her moose as she drank. But as soon as she finished, she began to cry again.

Doug pretended to make the moose speak, but that scared Dirtbike. She cried harder. He

pulled out every toy she owned,
but she wasn't interested. He ran
into the kitchen and grabbed
another bottle.

"Bah-bah," cooed Doug.

Dirtbike cried, but she took the
bottle. Several times, she drank a
little, then stopped and cried. She
started playing with the bottle.
Doug didn't care. He sat and

watched as she somehow pried
the top right off the bottle.
Formula spilled everywhere!
Doug ran to get paper towels.
Dirtbike giggled, playing in the
wet, milky mess.

As Doug cleaned up, the phone
rang. He answered, still holding
the baby.

"Hey, man. Honk, honk!" Skeeter greeted him. "Are you ready for some serious goofing off at the mall?"

"I can't," Doug told him. As he spoke, he got another bottle. "I've got to stay here and baby-sit Dirtbike while my mom picks up my grandma at the airport."

"Too bad, man. I just heard that Briar Langolier is signing autographs at the food court," Skeeter said.

"Can you get me one, Skeet? I'm stuck here," Doug complained.

"Sure, man. See ya!" Skeeter hung up.

Doug stooped to pick up the

bottle Dirtbike had dropped. As
he stood, she spit up all over both
of them.

"Aghh, gross!" Doug groaned,
feeling queasy. He headed for the
bathroom to take the baby's
clothes—and his shirt—off. Just
as he got her changed, she spit
up again.

Doug was desperate. He put
Dirtbike down and speed-dialed
the Skeeter Help Line.

"Help!" cried Doug. "She's
turned into a nonstop throw-up
machine!"

"*Wah!*" cried Dirtbike.

"When my baby brother gets
like that, my mom always takes

him places," said Skeeter. "Maybe
Dirtbike wants to go see Briar
Langolier at the mall."

"I don't know, Skeet," Doug
hesitated. "Judy said—"

At that second, Porkchop
barked and Doug looked up to see
Dirtbike, pulling at the lace table-
cloth under the lamp. "Ahhhhh!"
he screamed, dropping the phone

and racing to catch the lamp. He picked up the baby and ran back to the still-swinging phone.

"Skeet? Are you still there?" he asked.

"Sure, man. What happened?" asked Skeeter.

"Never mind. We've got to get out of here before she destroys the whole house!" declared Doug. "We'll swing by your place so we can walk together."

CHAPTER SIX

Skeeter and Doug chatted as they walked to the Four-Leaf Clover Mall. Porkchop strolled alongside the baby. Doug had managed to get her dirty clothes off, but now she was dressed only in her diaper.

Porkchop stopped and pointed to her. She was asleep.

"Great!" Doug said. "Now we

won't have any trouble getting Briar's autograph! Judy was wrong. This was a great idea."

But the moment they entered the mall, some kid popped his balloon. Dirtbike woke up and began to cry.

"Give her a toy, Doug," suggested Skeeter.

"I forgot to bring one," gulped Doug. She cried louder. "This is definitely an emergency," he declared, taking out the twenty dollar bill.

They hurried to the toy store. Dirtbike saw a life-sized moose and tried to reach for it. "Un, uh," she grunted.

"No, Dirtbike, I don't have enough money for that one," Doug told her.

Dirtbike did not care. She wanted that one.

"Try this," Skeeter said, handing Doug a green and purple squiggly snake.

Dirtbike hugged the snake, then

threw it to the floor. Doug paid for it and they left.

"I hope we find Briar soon," said Skeeter.

"Me, too," Doug said, picking up Dirtbike's snake. He handed it to her.

Just then, Porkchop barked. He saw Briar Langolier! A huge line led to her table.

They stood in line a few minutes, taking turns picking up Dirtbike's snake. Dirtbike laughed at the Pick Up the Snake game.

"This isn't so bad," said Doug.

Skeeter sniffed. Something smelled funny. . . .

"Ah, Doug, I think Dirtbike needs a new diaper," he said.

Doug caught a whiff, too. "P.U!" His mind drifted as he imagined himself wearing a hazardous material suit with big rubber gloves, holding a very stinky baby

sister. Sirens screamed. "Warning! Warning!" someone shouted from a hovering helicopter. "Nuclear stink bomb attack! Run for your lives!"

Around him, everyone ran in all directions.

"Doug? Doug? Are you all right?" said a familiar voice, ending his daydream.

"Oh, hey, Patti. Hey, Beebe. We're waiting to see Briar," he said, hoping they wouldn't notice the smell.

"Phew! What stinks?" said Beebe as she pinched her nose.

"Doug, I think Dirtbike needs a diaper change," Patti said.

"Uh, yeah, I better deal with it right away," Doug agreed, blushing. "Skeeter, get me an autograph, if you can. See ya."

CHAPTER SEVEN

Now, it's me against the diaper, thought Doug, heading for the men's room. I should have listened to Judy.

A minute later he stood in the bathroom with the stroller, looking for a good changing spot. "What do you think, Porkchop?"

Porkchop made an "I don't know" noise.

Doug went back in the mall and stood, trying to decide what to do. Dirtbike was crying again. Porkchop tickled her with the snake. This time, it didn't work. Doug wished he could ask someone for advice.

"DOUG! WHAT ARE YOU DOING HERE?"

Judy was angry. More angry than Doug had ever seen her.

He tried to explain. "Dirtbike wouldn't stop crying! She kept throwing up, and I didn't know what to—"

"So you brought her to the

mall? Genius, Doug! Real genius!
Look, she's practically naked!"
She sniffed. "Ugh! And her diaper
is dirty! I thought you said you
could change her!"

"I was going to," Doug said, "but
where do I put her down?"

"Give her to me, amateur! You are so undependable! You can't even be trusted with the simplest baby-sitting tasks! And now you have humiliated me in the middle of Bluffington's most public place!"

Judy took Dirtbike from Doug. Her voice changed. "Come here, my little precious! Does Judy's little sweet-ums want her di-dee changed? Let's get you out of this nasty old mall! Judy will fix everything," she cooed.

When she turned to Doug, her tone changed again. "Okay, Goofball. Get her stuff. Let's go."

CHAPTER EIGHT

"Aargh!" screamed Judy at home. Toys were everywhere. Empty bottles were in the middle of the floor. Wet, sticky towels hung all over the kitchen. Dirtbike's dirty clothes and spit-up covered the bathroom floor. The house was a mess.

"What happened in here, Doug?" Judy asked.

"A lot!" he answered. "It's not *my* fault! *You* were supposed to stay here, too!"

"Well, if you think you're getting paid for this disaster, you can just think again!" Judy hollered. "You are determined to ruin my life, aren't you? The least you could do was clean up before you left home! Oh, you are so caught, Dougie!"

"Well, you're just as caught as I am!" he yelled back. "In fact, when Mom gets—" Suddenly he stopped. OH, NO! MOM!

Judy looked at him. She remembered, too. Mom would be home soon with Grandma Opal. If they found things like this, Doug and Judy would be grounded for life!

Desperate times called for desperate measures. Doug took a deep breath.

"Look, Judy, I'm sorry I blew it. But this is a huge mess. We have to work together. Team?" Doug asked.

"Team, little brother," she answered. Porkchop jumped in the air like a cheerleader.

They began Operation Cleanup. Even Dirtbike got

into the act. Doug tied washcloths
on her hands and knees. Then he
turned her loose. As she crawled
around, she left the floor sparkling
behind her.

No sooner had they finished
cleaning than they heard the car
pull up. Mom was home!

CHAPTER NINE

Grandma Opal sat at the kitchen table with her leg up on a stool, eating cookies and drinking milk with Theda, Judy, Dirtbike, Doug, and Porkchop.

"Theda, your house is so neat and clean," Grandma Opal declared. "How do you do it?"

Doug and Judy looked at each other.

"Well, Mom, the kids did a wonderful job!" Theda praised them. "They're the best kids in the world!"

Judy looked at Doug. He nodded. Better get it over with now. She said, "Well, actually, Mom, we did have a little excitement. . . ."

When they finished telling the whole tale, they were grounded for two weeks—plus Doug had several joint baby-sitting appointments with Judy so she could teach him how to handle Dirtbike.

Grandma Opal said, "Doug, I should have come to visit you instead of skiing in Yakestonia! A day with you and Dirtbike sounds exciting."

"Well," Doug said, "I did learn a lot. Taking care of a little baby is a *big* job!"

Judy chimed in. "And we should have done what Mom and Dad said. Then we wouldn't be grounded. Besides, the ice melted at 'Shakespeare on Ice'—turning *Romeo and Juliet* into *The Tempest!*"

Grandma Opal chuckled at Judy's obscure Shakespeare joke.

In her high chair, Dirtbike

cried. Doug ran over and picked
her up.

Dirtbike looked straight at
Doug and held her arms out to
him. "A-Duh!" she said.

Everyone laughed.

Grandma Opal was surprised.

"Did you hear that? She said *Doug*!"

"She said my name?" Doug said happily, taking her and hugging her tightly. "She *really* said my name!"

THE ONLINE SERVICE FOR KIDS

- **PLAY** fast paced games against live opponents.

- **SOLVE** online mysteries & steer the action in loads of different interactive stories.

- **DESIGN** party favors & other SUPER FUN activities.

- **SEND & RECEIVE** exciting, animated e-mail.

- **AND MUCH, MUCH MORE!**

TRY IT FREE TODAY!

FOR A ONE MONTH FREE TRIAL,

go to **www.disneyblast.com/doug**

or skip the download and get your FREE CD-ROM by

calling toll-free **1(888) 594-BLAST today!**

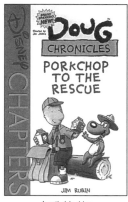

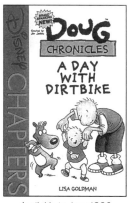

Created by
Jim Jinkins

Doug, Patti, Skeeter, Soft Friends From Mattel!